Songs From A San Diego Morning

c. a. lindsay

Creative Commerce
Carlsbad, California

First Printing
© Carol Ann Lindsay 1993
American Book Concepts
Texas

Second Printing
With additional poems
©by Carol Ann Lindsay 2007
Printed in the U.S.A.
by Lulu Books
North Carolina

Grateful acknowledgment to the following publications in which these poems previously appeared:

Old Hickory Review, Jackson Arts Council TN: "Rainbow" and
     "A Snail"
Mobius, Magazine of The Orion Art Center, Michigan: "San Diego
     Snowman"
The New Press Literary Quarterly NY and *Cornucopia*, Moose Bound Press,
     Anchorage AK: "Goal"
Spirit Dancer Magazine, Springfield MO and *The Poet's Pen*, Upper
     Room Publishing GA: "One Free Wind"
Limestone Circle, a Literary Quarterly and *Wide Open Magazine*, CA:
     "Cuyamaca Peak"
USA TODAY newspaper 12/20/91: "The Crooked Tree"
Writer's Exchange, Society Hill SC: "The Other Side of Fog"
Legion of Light Magazine, NY: "The Best" and "Bitter Water"
Memories Poetfest, Middletown NY and *Red Bluff News*, Redbluff, CA:
     "One Gift"
Z Miscellaneous, NY: "Cactus"
Lynx Eye, Scribblefest Literary Group, Los Angeles: "The Gray Marble
     Buddha"
So Luminous The Wild Flowers, Tebot Bach, CA, *The Kit-Cat Review* NY:
     "For My Girl Who Died Too Young" ("Candice Andromeda")
Leatherneck, magazine of the Marines: "Iwo Jima"
Down Peaceful Paths, Quill Books, TX: "Grass" and "My Father"
Slate and Style, Magazine of the National Federation of Blind Writers,
     NY: "Lost Hills"
Write Touch, WA and *The Centerfold*, West End Theatre, NYC: "I Loved
     Him"
The New Press Quarterly, NY: "goal"
Fast Food Blues, Moose Bound Press AK: "happy hour"
A Celebration of Poets, Poetry Guild, OH and *Red Bluff News*,
     CA 3/19/97: "church"
2003 NW Cultural Council Art Exhibition, ILL: "Seeing Everything"
     Voices in Wartime, Poets Against The War, Port Townsend WA:
     "Acquainted With Grief"
The Poet's Pen, Society of American Poets, GA: "The Best," "Bridge,"
     "God's Mudpie," and "The Birds"
Poetry Break Journal, "Navy Pilot"
Big Two-Hearted, Secord Press, Upper Peninsula Library, MI: "Drain"
Katrina's Poems, Central Louisiana Arts Council, LA: "Wild Winds"
The Pen Woman NLAPW magazine, D.C.: "Grass"
Tupelo Press Poetry Project July 2007: "Snail"

Contents

Part IV *From Life*

Part V *About Poetry and Other Things A California Poet*
        Thinks

Part I

From the Sea to the Mountains

San Diego Snowman

yesterday,
it rained quite hard
in San Diego air
sending surging waves that
elated surfers knew meant
snow on Mount Laguna,
which it did.

today,
some people sit
on the beach
facing east
where naked peaks
wear white,
while others from the city
make a pilgrimage
to shovel snow
into trucks
that take the winter home
so children of the sun
can have a snowball fight
and man with eyes of coal
on San Diego sod.

Rainbow

Sun caressed my neck
through glass in the car
at the same time
a cloud-capped rainbow
grew like elastic
in front of me.
I drove the freeway hill,
over sixty-five,
to find where it began
and spotted
the arc of many colors
stroking the valley.
The instant
I saw the rainbow
touch trees
and old buildings,
it vanished,
and I felt betrayed
by God.

One Free Wind

There is one ship that sails the sea,
Against a wind where I can be,
Away from mist and traps on land,
In space that sculpts a heavenly band.

The Captain at the wooden wheel,
Tips his hat so he can steal
A longing look at one white mast,
And two blue stacks in iron cast.

The rig sets sail through waves of blue,
Towards the horizon that gives a clue,
Of life beyond the matter of earth,
And living devoid of worldly worth.

When the deck is filled with a freedom song,
My soul's in a search of a place to belong,
Where like the breeze, it's free to roam,
Instead of all shackled in a body tomb.

When the ship drops anchor in open space,
A carol salutes that sacred place,
Where all of mankind wants to be,
Like magic wind waving and finally free.

Cuyamaca Peak

Cuyamaca Peak,
a voiceless space
of severed rocks,
pink manzanita,
and ocean view
exists near sky
in stainless stillness

          until a jet drones.

The Crooked Tree

How the whispering pine changes
faces; fragrant, full, fanned
by breeze of mountain ranges
adorning land on desert sand
waving needled hands
to offer nature's sigh
against a winter sky
where it breathes free
before the season's blasphemy:
a tinseled requiem and
painted fabrications - but
the stem arcs in space
that is the perfect place
to dress a house for Christmas
and ignore the child who asks,
"Why is the tree crooked
that stood so straight outside?"

The Other Side of Fog

How fog fades the mountain and
swallows the brutal gorge in white
haze: silent, blinding wall
that shades the truth until
sun melts the mocking mist
to let man know of light
and maybe even God
on the other side of fog.

G R A S S

Brushing a blade of grass
with my finger,
a plant
is dwarfed by my hand -
then an ant
crawls up its spine
and I see
how gargantuan
grass really is.

T u m b l e w e e d

Tumbleweed
is green and soft
until it matures
and wind rolls it round.

I Almost Gave Her Fifteen Cents

I almost gave her fifteen cents,
The homeless woman on the street,
Who was no bum, like ones I saw
Along the San Diego road.

I almost gave her fifteen cents,
The one who walked with jagged beat
And wore a dress and steely eye
That made her seem demented.

I almost gave her fifteen cents,
The day she asked in hot sun heat
Near vagrant men who were asleep
In car lots claimed as residence.

I almost gave her fifteen cents,
Though bribes decreed by tramps I meet,
Short shrift the folks who pay the graft
With dollars earned from honest work.

I almost gave her fifteen cents,
And then I saw her hands and feet
That cursed her with some others, too,
Because of Winstons and new shoes.

Homeless

Candice saw news about crime today
And homeless in line for bread near the bay,
Which drove my blond little girl to say,
"Hey, Mom, if we give all of our bread away
And money Dad works for day after day,
Then we can be homeless, without food and pay."

One Gift

A flower grew from seed,
soft and pungent smelling,
and it's free
for the mother hiding
truth about a shining
dandelion being weed.

The Birds

Candice threw crumbs
of old bread in the air,
with hopes that gray seagulls
would catch what she spread,
except the birds came
from the waves without warning
to snatch rotten rolls
she had placed on the sand.
And then they flew up
near her little hand,
making her laugh
at the squawking sea beggars,
who tugged for some food
from her brown empty bag.

Michael

My son, my firstborn child,
Gave me so much life,
At a time when days were wild,
And the world so full of strife.

He grew up playing music
In the band and in his room,
Holding a guitar pick,
To breed a roaring boom.

And when he was a student,
Who spoke against all war,
I could see the world was bent
With bureaucratic lore.

He talked about the killing,
That happens in a fight,
When young armed men are willing,
To see the rocket's light.

He walked in peace and saw a call
To join and follow rank,
Within a Guard where he stood tall
And served without a tank.

He learned to follow love
And find a place to be
Embraced by things above
Any fabricated human key.

And now that he's a father,
My son, the vegetarian,
Knows how much his mother,
Loves and cares for him.

The Best

He had chubby, baby hands when he threw his first ball,
And it went flying down the hall to hit hard on the wall,
In sight of one young mother, who divined a baseball arm,
And not a lad adept at throwing strikes upon the barn.

But as the boy grew taller, his arm got stronger, too,
And he mulled over baseball, not a cow that uttered moo,
Fleeing sometimes all his chores for ball upon the grass,
Which he practiced on the shed and caught in leather mass.

His arms and legs had bruises and scratches alike,
When the boy first put on shoes, he proudly said were spike,
And played a regulation field, lighted in the dark,
No longer just kids play, or a day in city park.

He practiced and he played for the famous yellow team,
As speedy Second Baseman, when scouts searched for the
                                                   cream,
And he was one selected as a special league All-Star,
Before he was old enough for whiskey in a bar.

For awhile he had Second, then later played at First,
Always sipping Gatoraide to quench his growing thirst.
Then, at last, it was time for him to tip his hat,
And swing at a fast pitch with his silver bat.

He was known as the best to run right past the short,
Laughing hard when he got back inside the dugout fort,
Where coaches who had known him and just how he could
                                                   run,
Often ended diatribes with "You can do it, son."

He used the body dive, the way Pete Rose once did,
To touch homeplate with his hands for the winning bid,
Knowing nothing in his life would ever be the same,
After playing with the others for wanted Series fame.

The team scored wins and losses when it played out on the
road,
Coming home without the glory, but with a lighter load,
Giving one young boy in Little League awareness of the
start,
Of something quite imposing in which he played prime part.

The game has ended now that the boy is twenty-five,
And though he never showed the pros his arm and Pete
Rose dive,
His mother knows without one doubt, he was the very best,
Of all the baseball arms she'd seen that ever passed the test.

For Mark, an El Cajon Little League All Star, who also played semi-pro ball. Mark is currently a teacher in the Cajon Valley School District, El Cajon, California and coach for Lakeside Little League, Lakeside, California.

Christine

I called her Christino, my little Bambino,
In the days that are long gone from this one,
When she was so tiny, my beautiful girl,
Wearing a crown of one little curl.

I look on those days when I rocked her so much,
Recalling the joy of her soft, gentle, touch,
Along with sleigh rides and long stroller walks,
On streets full of kids with pure baby talks.

At lessons she took at Miss Johnson's tap class,
Her toddler feet moved with the rapping of brass,
To stay with the rhythm of musical sound,
About Leroy, the man, the baddest in town.

She grew and she practiced the dance and keyboard,
While I, as her mother, happily soared
To contests regarded as perfectly great,
Though sometimes I tired when shows ran on late.

And though it now seems, she was just sweet sixteen,
The Christine who will always be my teen queen,
Now walks alongside of her own little girl,
And softly strokes future with bows on a curl.

Today, when I gave a stuffed toy to her boy,
I remembered the day she had left me, you see,
To follow her own path to flourishing joy,
Where she can be free and not someone's maybe.

Horse Chasers
(aka The Ambulance)

Candice laughed, and so did I,
As it passed quickly by,
The white and red machine,
Behind the Princess and Big Gus,
Friendly Blue and Gentle Queen,
Until a racetrack fuss
Came from Green Fifteen
Who showed up on the screen.

Then the bells rang out again
To start another race
With a pack of ten who ran
The track at a swift pace,
The ambulance behind them,
Until a horse named Purple Lace,
Touched the finished line.

Candice laughed and so did I
When it passed slowly by.

Del Mar Racetrack

At the Turf Club people dine
And drink some very fine wine

In clothing fit for kings,
Inside a covered grandstand

Where men wear ornate rings.
They sit behind cheap Terrace seats,

Where some sip beer in a lawn chair,
To watch the horses run,

And bet on which will win -
A perfect San Diego day

Where social classes are akin
And share the ocean breeze,

While they watch the seagulls fly,
Between green bluffs, the hill of trees,

And a humming Highway Five.

H o l i d a y

People leave the city
to find a sacred place
in mountain parks
and desert land,
or silent lakes
and ocean sand,
but radios
they bring along
drown the sound
of nature's song.

e a r t h q u a k e

sleeping, sleeping Sunday.

waking, waking, waking,

swaying, swaying, swaying,

cracking, cracking, cracking,

the longest, longest minute,

but I'd rather shake in San Diego
when an earthquake hits
than ride around Chicago
near truck drivers having fits.

Rain In July

Sun shines in December,
October and November,
so when a Summer rain
kissed the thirsty grass,
my child asked me why
a stormy symphony
would strike so blatantly.

We both could feel a greater fear
from glowing naked hills
inside the womb of night,
than from a rolling rumble
or the super shake
of a California quake.

As we watch the mystic sight
dance from left to right,
we ask a godly question
as we seek a solid answer
for the slander against nature
when it rains in July.

Stopping by Waves on a Rainy Morning

Whose waves are these, do you know?
Near the snug harbor where west winds blow?
The Captain can't see me standing here
Waiting for the angry storm to go.

The seagull doesn't show any fear
When I stand on a foggy dock with my gear.
It only stalks the rocks where I took
A walk one misty morning this year.

When he gives his white wings a shake,
I wonder if rain is a big mistake.
As the downpours come and daily sweep
The sand and the bluff that's supposed to sun bake.

The waves are ugly, green, and deep,
But I have no vows to keep,
And no place to go when the hillsides seep,
And no place to go when the hillsides seep.

Influenced by Robert Frost

Floral   With   A   Rose

The artist, in the sunrise,
Roamed a perfect place,
Where her knowing eyes,
Could view each part of space.

And then she took a brush,
Dipped in rainbow hues,
To mirror in the morning hush,
Exotic garden views.

She saw by midday sun,
Rich flowers fill her vase,
And shape what had begun
To exist as fragrant lace.

And by the daystar's final call,
A rose embraced the light,
Where black shadows never fall,
Because there is no day or night

for floral with a rose.

FLORAL WITH A ROSE was hung in the Drawing Room of Todd Lincoln's house, currently the Pen Arts Building in Washington, D.C. It was placed beneath the painting FLORAL WITH ROSE by artist Marian Spinn. The poem was specifically written for this artwork.

Black Widow

Fibers spun with dignity,
are blended surreptitiously,
and when the spider's work is done,
mankind's job has just begun
in space where dirt has won,
along with junk and toys of fun
which hide the cunning fatal trap,
the soft, seductive, woven map,
that is known without a doubt
as yoked to some malicious clout
when a spider dances out
searching for a place to go
for manna

               – sly black widow.

A Snail

A sneaky snail
with fatal feelers
slithered slyly
in the dark
to feed on
my Creeping Charlie,
and when I picked it up,
it hid
in the shell,
just as it did
in daylight:
a gift from France that did bestow
the New World with escargot.

NOTE: Creeping Charlie is a plant that grows readily in San Diego County, usually in a patio hanging planter.

CITY HERMIT

City people work
and then go home - free
from magic nights or
daylight rides and
ice cream cones - safe
from one old man
in a rocking chair
who stares
at mocking air,
but sees
the emptiness
that's there.

Jet Ski

Once, in the winter,
I walked a mile
in clean snow
to ski
and in summer
held a rope
behind a boat
to ride a crystal lake.
Today,
in winter fog
and summer smog,
my son
hauls a jet ski
to the bay
in his green truck
so he can skim
dirty water
and feel free -
his burden is light
compared to mine
and then I see
tomorrow will be
with a defiled sea.

The Swallows Came Back,
But First They Stopped At My Place

The rasping, twittering noise
echoed like a loose shutter in wind,

so I looked outside to see
black pointed, narrow wings fluttering

in circles. They flew segregated,
when they put mud and straw on the ledge

above my cathedral window,
just beneath the tile roof.

A trail to my front door
confirms the flocks vitality

and I wonder if the birds are lost.
This year weather changed,

and the creek flows like a river
spawning flies and gnats that

make famine disappear for birds,
and offers work to those

who cover my hacienda
with huge nets. If swallows

had space at my place,
I wouldn't need the pesticide man.

My house was a field last year
and it's March again. They say

the swallows always find the old church. Maybe,
when the nest is hosed down,

they'll find their way back
to San Juan Capistrano.

Are You The Coal Man's Son?

Are you the coal man's son,
The coal man of my mother,
Who drove a truck with a ton
From one street to another?

Are you the coal man's boy,
The coal man of Hoboken,
Who held with secret joy,
The words from blues eyes spoken?

Are you the coal man's heir,
The coal man of depression,
Who stood at mother's stair
To offer warm creation?

Are you the coal man's pride,
The man in coal bin holes,
Who shoveled coal inside,
While humming tunes of souls?

Are you the coal man's son,
Who lives near western shore,
And sings to me, a loving poem,
Connecting us once more?

In memory of Frank Sinatra whose father was my mother's
coal man in Hoboken, New Jersey during the 1930s.

bridge

the artificial frame
across a highway gorge,
gives one naked mountain
made of godly worth
connection to an architect
who lives on planet earth.

The Old Barn

The old barn, unused by man,
looking weak and fragile,
still sits stubborn in the wind
though leaning at an angle,
with broken boards
and worn white pain,
but a roof that lets in Heaven.

On The Way to Stonewall Peak

Stiff, naked
arms
reach to sky
and I
passed it by.

Pointed, ugly
fingers
bend to earth
and seem to be
devoid of worth.

Silent, silhouette
breathed
when I stopped
to see
life
in a dead tree:

> artist's perfect picture
> nest for humming bees
> new dirt for budding trees

smoke signal

funnels of smoke
fuse with the clouds
over a space
that once was a place
for an Indian race,
but today the gray signal
tells of a mill
making a chair.

Not Only God

A truck hauls
exhumed mountain
and a stone
hits my windshield
on the freeway.
Then I can see
how man can mold
what someone said
only God could shape.

Earth Birth

The mountain shaved
by the lumberjack
could still be saved
if one just man
put a seedling back.

Still Water

The lake is still
embraced by a hill
framing an image on water
of living rocks
on a naked peak,
until a soft breeze
brushes the air
and warps
the perfect picture.

An Old Man Walking

He holds his feet to the sidewalk
as some driving faster than his eyelids blink

pass him. His eyes catch stately trees
armed with lemons guarded by the stop sign

where a car horn punctures the morning.
He looks up and sneaks a peek at snow

on the mountain while he keeps moving,
glad to be in a place painted with flowers

in winter and trimmed with palm fronds
reigning over winds whipped up in the desert.

Under his hat, wrinkled skin embraced by the sun,
swings with each step. He can't see his bones

dissolving when he stops to sip coffee,
cheap with his senior discount card.

He has no mercy for terrible teens
who inherit polluted politicians

and air from him
as he reads the free newspaper

he is sure is pure
truth.

In the Spring, when the snowbird flies home,
he naps and recalls yesterdays that are suspended

perfectly.

A counterfeit resurrection
shelters him inside of a church

full of old people
who walk under the crumbling arches.

He has kept the faith,
but tries to save his body by feasting

on pills three times a day
paid for with taxes on the young

who are don't care -

       about an old man walking.

My Father

My Father, seventy-eight,
walked the California street.
He asked the name of plants
and I pointed to red apple
next to poisonous, purple
flowers of the oleander.
Then,
we hiked the hill of palms
and flowering cactus, too.
Dad looked at me,
trustfully,
expectant eyes widening
with surprise
that I knew what I knew.

Dancing on the Dark Side of Light

At Stonewall Mountain and Cuyamaca Peak,
the wind and trees slept together
night after full moon night
and day after sunlit day.
And in winter,
the forest shared the virgin snow
with children of the sun
who saw Sunrise Highway,
a windy road that waves at the sea.
Sometimes, in the rolling fog,
wind shuffled softly through the pines,
but one day, as the smoldering daystar bowed to the
                                                    east,
a Santana Wind blew up from the desert
and flames flooded the night with red light
plundering green needles that embroidered the hills
and stones. The fire screamed
with exploding manzanita and eucalyptus oil.
The forest that overflowed
with mountain lions, deer, and coyotes, fell silent,
and ashes left scents over the valleys
from the hills to the sea. Nothing,
but naked shadows on black, black earth
and gray, gray sky hung over wind
that threw up pieces of life everywhere,
even the city. There is no word for death
left behind a fire storm
that marched to the tune of sirens
until one water drop at a time and
one spray of pink retardant at a time
fell out of the sky to tuck in fires
that buried mornings, and afternoons
day after day after day until the silence came,

the silence that added up all the past
and future wonders of the city and mountains

that danced on the dark side of light.

In memory of the firefighter and all the people who died in the Cedar Fire, a fire that burned almost three thousand homes in San Diego County and the Cleveland National Forest, October 2003.

The Grunion Dance In C

In the middle of the night when the moon was very full,
I walked beside the sea in the shifting, sacred sand,
To await a shining lovefest when grunion lease the
                                                    land,
Routinely claimed at sunrise by mankind and the gull.

And just as waves exploded along the peaceful shore,
A herd of flitting sandpipers darted out with speed,
Sure the silver lovers would freely plant their seed,
At the instant that the high tide made its booming roar.

So deep into the night when the foaming torrent came,
A flashing fish weighed anchor in that exclusive place,
Where shadows hug creation above a private space,
When waltzing males encircle, one gleaming, upright
                                                    dame.

After that they came, with more tossing of the waves,
Many, many hundreds, who joined the revelry,
Until the waning tide could throw them back to sea,
After casting fertile eggs inside deep sandy caves.

For almost two dark hours I heard the music play,
With rare majestic chords of one fine symphony,
A serenade now known as "The Grunion Dance in C,"
Which beats the drums of darkness before the crown of
                                                    day.

NOTE: Grunion is a small fish in the coastal waters of
Southern California and Baja, California that spawns along
beaches during Spring high tides at the time of the full moon.
With the tide thousands line the beaches for an hour, then
return to the sea.   Lindsay has been a volunteer for the
Pepperdine University Grunion Project.

Freedom

In solitude,
a stalking speck,
bobbed in brisky breeze,
until the surfer sensed,
freedom's flaming core,
sweeping him to shore.

Sewage Spill

The warning on the waves
breaking near the shore,
hides the truth in fragile foam
when stinking sewage sweeps
to the shifting sand
that grips an orange sign
hammered on the beach
to keep a crime in line
and child from the slime.

control

in my claimed space
on stainless sand,
a perfect picture from the land
of rays with changing faces,
dance serenely on the sea
free of any worldly fee -
but the angry buzzing sound
of a black bee goes around me
and I miss the last design
when day runs to the finish line.

The Way Of The Flesh

He's alone and dying, barely raising his head
when the water he needs, falls over his mouth.
Nobody under the rain cares. They ignore him,

the black and brown ones who waddle by
without even looking up, some
holding their long necks high, and I wonder

about the silent voice that once gripped a barking,
guttural sound. Where's his family? Where
are his friends? As gray clouds hover, I remember

life he gave to scores, life that gives life
in the sea and out of it, and time, time he offered
to many who breathe free and feel the sun and

wind blowing with the cycles of cold and hot
seasons drenched with songs of the earth
that shatter evil with mystic chants. It was hard

for him to grow up because storms and
predators invaded the space around him.
When adulthood summoned, he

boldly defended the colony from
a cartel that would prey on his family. He
saved them from bondage and now I understand

his wild ways and eccentric existence were full
of vagrant liberty that gave him immunity from being
a caged piece of carnal flesh. Now rain pours over him

and he's free to die after living devoid of embargoes
on his desires. He finished sipping the cup
of life with other sea lions and is blind

to white and gray seagulls scouring the sand
for food near him. As gooney birds and
pelicans stalk him, he takes his last breath

and high tide presides over a proper burial.

Crystal

The name that was given when she was born,
Had no intention of a soul being torn
Between life and death for a whole life-time,
But someone adorned with sparkle and shine.

Crystal, a virgin who was and will be,
Forever a guest of the wrinkled sea,
Steps her feet softly on sand at the shore,
Reflecting today on what's at her life's core.

Everything started when she was a teen
In love with life and all that would seem
Open, alive, with tomorrows unknown,
Eager to launch a world of her own.

But all of it ended when she was sixteen,
And evil pervaded the sylvan scene,
Stealing from her the first love she had
In a drowning the news said simply was sad.

The tears that had fallen so long ago,
Are still in her soul, a silent woe,
As shapes of the image she still wants to reach
Come near the water along the south beach.

Her body looks old to all of the young,
When whispers of love come out from her tongue,
And empty eyes stare at the chainless sea,
In search of a dream that might yet still be.

I Sat at the Sea

I sat at the sea
Just to be with me
And thoughts about life
And infinity.

I watched a straight line
Beyond the green brine
Connected to sky
As a holy shrine.

But a ship changed the scene
Meant to be serene
And took the perfection
From where I had been.

It dipped in a wave
That created a cave
With the magic of water
Sprinkled to save.

Then a ray dance
Revealed a new glance
At truth marking evil
And earth's last chance.

Wild Winds
2005

From my window, I see Eucalyptus trees
bend in the ocean breeze and watch the gray dove
find a place on the fence.   The water runs fast
over dishes in the sink and I think
about words I hear on my black plastic radio.
It's hard to believe, as I remember the tremor
that shook the ground here,
and the rain, the winter rains that came
last year. In the rain, the sidewalk near my house
moved to the middle of the road.   It still moves
near houses that crack as the hillside crumbles.
The people had to leave,
but they had sun after the rain,
while the people of Katrina had nothing
but streets and houses
full of dark, polluted, stinking water.
Two years ago, the Devil Winds
pushed a fire through our canyons
and mountains. Young mothers and teens,
burned in their cars on the way out
and three thousand houses were cremated.
Few people across America helped the people
here.   Some of the victims still live in trailers,
the way the people of Katrina will live two years
from today.   The holes in my heart
that came after my husband
and 16 year old Candice died,
stretched out for the people
of the storm who lost their families,
their friends,
and their homes.

*

When more wild winds come
to steal souls in the South,

I wonder

if

God

is.

I know there is

one thing waiting for them -

the gift

of time.

Written for Beyond Katrina, a book produced by the Arts Council of Central Louisiana with proceeds donated to benefit hurricane victims

Iron Mountain

The black,
twisted soldiers
stand still in a row
on hills
sterilized by fire.
Today,
hawks squawk
and stalk
dead vegetation
consumed by flames
last year.
At the foot of each sentinel,
green sprouts
prove that manzanita
never die
along the path
to Iron Mountain.

Forest Fire

A city is created
from wood on northern trees,
and mankind is neglected
by guards of birds and bees -
today one thousand houses
and a fragrant, fertile forest
burned in mountain breeze
near a place the law decrees
that logging is excluded
to save bird habitation
which now is extant
as black and lifeless ashes.

Lost Hills

Hundreds of pumping oil wells
secure upon a hill,
far from mankind and the sea,
signed by a giant monopoly,
pilfers a resource
offered by earth,
and then leaves steel fists
to rot in the sand.

Grapevine

The withered winter vine
with naked, knotted branches
nailed to man-made fences,
chains the cursing crosses
for the men who drink fine wine.

Part II

From the Desert

Cactus

The prickly green tower,
A crooked desert vine,
Holds a flaming tongue
Towards the spangled sun
To shroud just one betrayal
Of wasteland beauty won
In sand with golden rays -
A piece of nature
Left untouched
Because of needled spine
That hints of evil devil
In one holy design.

Bitter Water

How the cool water changes desert
with a naked trick; clean, clear
cascading from fingers, but
bitter on a thirsty tongue
that uncoils with a jeer
at God's neglect
of salvation here.

God's Mudpie

Mounds of sterile soil
with rocks and cactus plants,
form impressions
that appear
to show God's fingers
once played here.

desert chimes

in the silent morning sky,
the raven finds a dragon fly,
and just below it, on the sand,
where black, black spiders crawl,
a sacred rattlesnake,
warns intruders of the land
that desert chimes will ring for man.

Desert Boat

A sailboat in the desert
On a trailer truck,
Moves faster on the highway
Than on a windy sea -
On land it gives man a job,
In water, time to be.

Desert Flower

Green leaves embracing
white and purple petals reaching
to the sky along a desert road,
would be a fine bouquet
for the dining table,

except the bloom is poison.

Light

Artificial light
ignites the desert night
with a pagan sight
that mocks the solar white.

d e s e r t   l i f e

lifeless sand
on windless

             land

in static summer heat

                  entombed

by jagged peaks
and naked rocks

                      breathes

in scoffing silence
until a snake
or lizard
sneaks from tumbleweed

                        to offer

proof
of desert packed with

                          life.

The Ghost of Calico

It wasn't long ago
When a thousand miners came,
To strike it rich in Calico,
Where silver was the game.

They brought their guns along
With cowboy boots and dreams
That often ended in a song
Beneath hot desert beams.

The midday heat came down
Like fire from above
To strike each lonely man in town
With lust for a woman's love.

The red sands on the hilly street
Formed clouds of dirty dust,
In shootouts that were seen as just
Inside the mesa heat.

But for a moment, fighting ceased,
The day a stagecoach came,
With a new girl from the East,
Who gave them all her name.

Kelly wore a dark blue shawl
When she came to town,
As her eyes spoke of a call
To life beyond sundown.

The men all came, of course,
To the gilded place,
Where Kelly was the source
Of all the happy space.

And after that, the drunkeness,
And fights inside dark mines,
Was blamed on brothel lewdness,
Not loss of silver finds.

But then one night, while she sang,
A gun was aimed at Kelly,
And the mocking sound that rang,
Touched every heart and belly.

Then, as she drew her last breath,
Every miner knew
His contribution to her death
Was on his conscience, too.

There was no stone to mark the grave
Where Kelly would be laid,
Since only those whom God would save,
Could have a marker made.

So in Calico one day,
The miners took her casket
Along the crooked pathway
To the hill above the city.

And when they laid the coffin down,
The church bells started clanging,
While gray clouds cast a frown,
And offered a strange banging.

The men, who heard the haunted sound,
Looked upward to the sky
With certainty that they had found
A loving woman's sigh.

From that day on, the men at night,
Would see her dance and sing
Beyond the end of daylight
When they were finished mining.

like the sun

life stopped when he left me
and my little girl to be alone
with death's distilled desertion
leaving my soul dry as the desert
wind, offering images of love
in a mirage that ends
only
when sunset shatters day -
at last
time dissolved
the shadows of yesterday
and a man
with soft lips turned future
the way morning sun
rebuffs the night.

Baby Doves

The chirping from the nest
Hidden in the trees,
Radiates with tiny pleas
Through soft, desert breeze,
Until mankind achieves
The quest to plant a dome
Upon the gray dove's home,
So man can be alone
And bitterly complain
Of noise from an airplane
That are driving him insane.

Roadrunner

A steel blue head
with bronze plumage,
and a sweeping tail,
suspiciously
surveys the land,
while scrawny legs
take bold steps
in front of me,
flaunting certainty
about his invisibility -
except I saw
the cocky, noiseless bird
with useless wings
who kills a rattlesnake
but cannot fly.

Valley Wind

When the valley wind blows,
tumbleweeds roll fast
while dead alfalfa bows
and man is surely blinded
by sweeping sand gusts
speeding through the air
which mock a truth of desert
about one clean atmosphere.

A Cowboy's Girl

I was a cowboy's girl,
In the wild west,
Waiting for the day he'd swirl
Me in the air upon his chest.

Every time he left me,
Tears rained down his shirt,
Because sweet love could never be
When cattle roamed the dirt.

Then one day he took the trail,
That led to danger's edge,
And the man who couldn't fail
Rode from a rocky ledge.

Of course they hunted for my man,
Along the steep ravine,
But when they looked, the horses ran
From the haunting scene.

The cowboys on the range with him,
Swore he didn't die,
When his horse slipped from the rim,
Because they saw him in the sky.

They saw a halo on his head
And grin around his face,
As he wandered from the dead,
And rode a godly pace.

The story grew as time went by,
And cowboys rode the range,
To prove his end was just a lie,
Devoid of heavenly change.

But on this day, as I look back
To love that once was mine,
I see him with his blue knapsack,
Full of kisses and old wine.

California Oak

Man has changed the land
that once was desert sand
and offered new creation
on the crest of flattened hills -
        a row of pink apartments.

The tumble weed that crowned the earth
was razed for stucco homes of worth
and soft, green vegetation
around the perfect rills -
        thick green sod.

The air is dry in this space
but oak trees from another place
are live from irrigation
through the desert chills -
        a golf course decoration.

And when a drop of rain
hits the window pane
with a windy invitation
that christens tile roofs -
        there is absolution
        for the tears of God
        on California oak.

Palm Tree Safari

When noble giraffes
Caged between hills,
Mingle with dancing green fronds
Under a sun that kisses brown ponds
Full of dull hippos and rhinos
Guarded by birds with yodeling bills,
The artist can hear
The call of the park
And paints waltzing trunks
Under green wands,
She calls a Palm Tree Safari.

*Written for "Palm Tree Safari," a painting by
award winning San Diego artist Jane La Fazio*

Drought

Shasta Lake is low this year,
Much lower than the last,
Existing as a cosmic jeer
That mocks the recent past
When winter came devoid of snow
And Spring had meager rain,
Giving Summer boats a chance
Before the storm rain dance.
The rhythm and the tune
Played near thirsty trees
To fill the water hole
And shun the deadly fees
For water from the lakes
That offers San Diego
Drinks and swimming pools
Along with water bills
That give the people chills,

But Shasta Lake is low this year,
Much lower than the last.

Part III

From the Days of My Grief

I L o v e d H i m

He loved me. More than anyone ever loved me.
By freeing my soul. He knew my unscrupulous
exploits, and if I was sad, or mad, or glad,
he was there. He asked for my Christmas list
and I wrote, "a baby." In the Fall Candice
was born. Then he bought a computer
and took our baby to the park
so I could write about birds and the trees
We talked and walked. Every day. We traveled
to the Grand Canyon, Yellowstone Park,
North Carolina and the Space Needle.
There are tools in the garage near bikes
and bike racks.   We knew all the trails
in San Diego. He was a good lover. Sometimes,
we sat still and heard wind wash the world
in the desert or on a rocky hill.
Every Sunday food was great
because he cooked. He was there
for Little League and soccer games;
for dance, piano and skating lessons.
At recitals he was a proud father.
He could tell a joke and I laughed.
Today, I was thinking about him.
For many years he was my best friend
and I loved him; but life changed
last year when he died.
Candice was eleven; I was forty-seven
but time will never steal good memories.

In memory of George Franklin Lindsay 1937-1992

c l e a n   s h e e t s

you had to leave,
and I loved you,
so I didn't change the sheets
until today
when I hugged the pillow
scented with your sweat,
yanked the blankets
from the bed, and
tore white linen
from the place
where you had slept with me.

then, I wrapped the covers
into a crooked ball,
but as I stuffed them in the tub
to wash your love away,
I smelled them once again
so I can feel your soul tonight
when I slip
between clean sheets.

Death

Poe had loved his Annabel Lee,
In the way that you had known me,
And now I just sit alone at the sea,
Because I was raped by death's cold key.

The raging waves break where I poured tears
On silver sand for over two years,
And cursed all creation for the bitter jeers
That sucked in the breath of Hell's secret fears.

The empty tomorrows and my endless grief,
Abrogated words meant to offer relief,
With swollen phrases about the belief
That pain can vanish like a blowing leaf.

Today, at the beach, I silently recall
Seductions of a life when I had it all,
And glowed with a smile inside a mortal wall
Where you were alive and walking quite tall.

Yes, Poe had loved his Annabel Lee
The way you had once loved me,
And now when I sit and gaze at the sea,
I still love life, but not it's death fee.

g o a l

in bed alone
with a silent phone,
yesterday explodes
with noisy children,
baseball games
and soccer,
PTA and lessons,
dirty dishes in the sink
and tender kisses
on the cheek
that are done
when love is gone -
she waits for a reason
to get out of bed
when a beeping truck
signals of life
beyond the garbage dump.

happy hour

they came, and so did I,
to be happy and feel connected,
so here we sit drinking
water, beer, and wine, looking
at red eyes, hearing
voices and a drum beat, talking
with counterfeit words, hoping
for intimacy; then we leave
full of empty dreams
and alone.

Widow At The Sea

The widow, staring at the sea,
her mind carving stony souvenirs
that can't be broken

like the wave massaging her bare feet,
is condemned to silent loneliness
and stinging tears.   Her salty flow

is swallowed by sand,
she hypnotically sifts
with her ringless hand. She cannot hear

the seductive surf song. Not even
the burst of screaming gulls
can sever the paralysis of her soul.

She looks beyond broken clouds
and chaining swells, but cannot see
the sun emerge. Then,

a child's sandcastle is nullified
by high tide,
and lost intimacy

is recast in her memory.

At The Beach

At the beach, lovers
watch the waves and kiss
near me. I want them

to know love
can be washed away,
but they are like

sea cucumbers
shackled in a tide pool
at sundown, waiting

for moon to
magnify the sea
with misty lunar rays

that sweep the minutes,
the way a magician
takes a long rope and

makes it short. When
surging swells sing,
it's time

for love to wear
the perfect catch
it cannot keep.

I wish they would leave
and stop reminding me
of what I forgot

about a man
who gave love
and died at dawn

before we could finish
dreams we had drafted
for our blond little girl.

church

they walk
through ornamented doors
and sit
girdled by stained glass
that filters Godly light.

they sing hallelujah
and hear about sin
and God
and love.

they pray
for the world
and then vacate the pew
to live beyond suffering
and a lonely woman
who follows them
silently out.

Storm Poem

When the storm hit,
I held my little girl's hand
and ran on the sand,
leaving footprints
for the tide to steal.
I didn't think about time
or the shadow of death
near her.
I only saw clouds
waving good-bye.

A Sea Breeze Blew In My Window

A sea breeze blew in my window
over the kitchen sink
tickling my face,
tossing my hair,
and dancing
on my eyelids,
reminding me
of once upon a time
when a child listened
to sea stories.
Today, everything
I smell is pungent
and all I feel
is a callous wind
I cannot share
since death
took you away.

Seeing Everything

I knew everything
when I was young,
about a snowman
alone in the cold
and a sandcastle
thawed by the tide,
but I didn't notice you
dancing on the line
with my clothes.

Then, ripened children
ambushed the rays of life,
and I moved to a place
brimming with clouds
and soldiers
marching to war.

In the fog, I watched
stars and stripes
drape coffin after coffin
to the tune of Eternal Father
while ashes of the flag
were blowing in
the flower child wind.
Everything
shattered the picture
for me where I sat
on the curb
under you
waving Old Glory
as veterans passed.

For awhile,
I saw you beat down
on migrant workers
in the lettuce patch,
and hover like an angel
over my baby
on a swing.

Then, everything changed
again. Today, I needed you
and felt something
that never deserted me,
even when darkness
stole the light from my life.

Some people say
that God shines on us,
but I only see
this side of the sun.

Acquainted With Grief

I have been acquainted with grief,
and it seemed to me that God nodded,
the way it seems he does when people rot
in war or famine. But I wasn't the only one asking
why towers soaring to heaven tumbled and crumbled
in a shuddering flame in the name of a god
who didn't seem to notice where God really was
or that some souls flew to the hands of Angels
at the same time others found the Devil's Paradise.
When the stillness of the morning was interrupted
by bent steel frames and human sod,
truth was exposed about pillars of strength
against the wind and rain. On that day
when a mother and child, a husband, a wife,
a father, a cousin, or brother disappeared,
the story came to me of a man named John
who was righteous, but lost his head because of a lie,
and one called Buddha who thought he found Nirvana.
God, who could blow all of the wickedness away,
didn't. Maybe, love can strangle the terror
and the hate. Maybe,

>   by seeing the spirit of darkness take a stand
>   everyone asleep on earth's land
>   can wake up and see the fight is about evil
>   that hides in us so that we can drive it
>   to the house of death. Then,
>   we can know of another place
>   where there is space
>   to have faith, hope
>   and the Greatest Love
>   and we can be
>   *free at last.*

Before The Coyotes Came

Before the coyotes came,
the world hung its coat in a far away land,
and the only waltz I knew
came from sea wind dancing on my nose
as breezes stole through the kitchen screen.

*

Before the coyotes came,
salvation was executed by ice plant
breeding on the hill in the yard. But one day,
the green succulent full of purple flowers,
mocked summer fires that burned a house
down the street. At night the bloom closed
and the door was open to a sports landscape
that was alive inside the decade's womb.

*

Before the coyotes came,
but after the bulls ran in Tecate,
I took a ripe breath and the moon melted
against the mountains in the morning light.
In the blazing sunrise,
I thought about creation coming,
and tasted a holy day
that was sweeter with each hour.
My voice resonated with a song
matching the pairing of birds
in our Eucalyptus tree.
The scent of fallen leaves
awakened sleeping pangs in me
while phantom angels hugged my spirit

under noon's daystar.
Life scorned evil then,
and when the sun left,
I held one still September night
between solid walls
and heard the chant of a divine list
as my body struggled
with the work of motherhood.
Then, the tiny heart of living flesh
beat next to my trembling arm
as my baby slumbered,
her face inclined toward my breast,
and her fingers curled like a rosebud.
The rustle of kissing and whispering
couldn't explain this union with my soul
which grew so fast days disappeared
into a blossoming darkness
that swallows the past. But I still remember
what she loved and that she played
"tackle decider" with her brother
before feeding the possum her cat's food.
Before the moon burned, Midnight's pellucid eyes
escorted her on the swing in the fenced yard
armed with future looming over toys
and a plastic Cabbage Patch house.
I stood in line three hours for a doll she adopted
and loved a fraction compared to my love for her.
After sun bleached her blond locks pure white,
we stood behind a zoo cage
where the coyote cast a stony stare into space,
then marched away to find a hiding place.
Her bright, blue eyes looked up,
and I felt more awake than any rabbit
or black cat stalking our neighborhood
before the coyotes came.   Birth and death

were protected by the feast of future
as time grew with a girl
who tempted rattle snakes
with her bike wheels.
The desert stuttered when we passed
perfect poison blooms
on our way to the wild canyon
where lightening inhabited our moments
while the world sucked up destruction
we didn't see. Words curled my tongue
when she won trophies
in the skating rink and soccer field.
Snails passed in the night leaving trails
for her to ponder and trimming her soul with magic
as she wondered where the sneaky slug
with fatal feelers had gone.
The algae in the fish pond
(where she filled her dump truck)
was as thick as the stock market
was devoid of eternal life.
I strolled with love across the meadow,
hearing the gully sing
during the covenant
made in spring
with a child who made
our family indivisible
before the coyotes came.

Keep Off The Grass

Velvet grass hemmed
with stainless, floral skirts,
gild the yards
where fathers pay
in time and sweat
each Saturday
for the children
called to play,
but not on perfect sod.

Pushing The Mower One Sunny Day

Pushing the mower
one sunny day,
I wondered why people
would want a machine
that pollutes fresh air,
mocks a quiet street,
robs a black resource,
and steals exercise
man buys for a fee
inside of a gym.

F r o g

Two years ago, my little girl
found a baby frog near the river,
and she brought it home
to love it in a box
and stroke it like a mother,
until she saw
a frog should be free,
and she let it go,
wondering for awhile
if the frog was alive.

Today tuneless croaking
called me outside,
where I saw it leap,
and then I knew why
there were holes in my leaves.

I Heard The Coyotes Cry

The thick, soft, tawny coat
had a muzzle pointed like a wolf's,
aimed northward on the street
next to the canyon. It seemed
a car had hit man's best friend
until I saw the black-tipped tail.
Then I felt no grief because
long, loud, whines in the dark
come when cats disappear
and coyotes celebrate lunch.
It's been two weeks since Midnight,
my little girl's cat vanished,
so I'm glad one of them is dead.
Maybe tomorrow I'll remember
my house stands on coyote land
and savor sounds of the night again.

Do Coyotes Eat In Rain?

Do coyotes
Eat in rain?
She asked
When we saw clouds
Creeping down
And felt rain
Dance on our skin.
We smelled the air
Slithering
Into our sore throats
Near the creek
That flows like a river
In the canyon
Where rabbits run,
Frogs croak a vulgar song,
And coyotes whine in the dark.
Tonight,
There was no wild
Sound around
Or even snail
To accidentally murder
On the wet ground,
And I couldn't tell her
If coyotes ate lunch
In the rain.

Evicted Dove in the Canyon

I want to fly free of yesterday
and unite with the flock
that passes over people in the canyon,
but tomorrow is stolen by a bulldozer.

I hunt for a tree to dream in
when smells from a chimney
scorch my desire.

I feel wind push me to a hill
where my perch is a transformer
that buzzes and burns my congregation.

I see the sun vanish
and hope for a parish
just as a jolt activates me
and I migrate to a dirty dumpster
to beg for free food.

seaweed

the chanting shadow sways
along the ocean floor,
until the current jerks the kelp
and washes it to shore,
where the olive, dead, design
of seaweed is a treasure
for the child who grabs the spine
that fills her life with pleasure

christening

like champagne in a crystal glass,
fermented, fizzling foam
christens a girl's sandcastle
with cool, curling water
that disappears
into the blooming tower
until the tide's
rebellious slap
robs the perfect work
of one
three foot tall creator.

The Gray Marble Buddha

There is no pulse on the gray marble Buddha
she bought from a thrift store and put on worn lace
made with gold threads by an old lady.

On top of her dresser, the solid carved rock
is blind to the night and day's mystic light
rays aimed through the window.

Her Buddha is cold
when memories defrost
as my fingers sweep dust
from a counterfeit god
embraced by teen treasures.

Buddha once faced her
with friends and alone
in minutes that slumber
with yesterday's dream. Sometimes,

loud music girdled the Buddha
with ears sealed in stone. Sometimes,
the room scented with popcorn
or candles in old brass holders,
quivered with life,
but the long nose of Buddha
stands as sterile as the ICU
where I guarded a piece of my soul.

Today, I hold Buddha in my hand
and there are no miracles.

I put Buddha down and
think about how far away planet earth is
from any perfect place.

For My Girl Who Died Too Young

I save my tears when they say
your body mangled in a car wreck
may not breathe tomorrow,
because you are a survivor.
Then, I let masked men take you
into the polished cathedral,
for expensive tattoos that run
from your throat all the way down.
You would savor the crooked design
conceived in a season cursed
with sleepless nights, sterile smells,
and "code blue" bells.

*

I watch the bed waiting,
(on the day of the Spring equinox,
when our hills are green
from Winter rain) and expect you,
my miracle child,
to wake up and say, "surprise."
Each second is eternity,
every minute, brutal time,
while acid pain inside of me
is fertilized with reality
when I learn what you knew
about the brain,
that it's the hard drive
for the mind which is the software
for the soul, which is the user.

*

I can't see the sun through fog
that devours me. I can't sense
time because dreams feast
on phantom flashes of life
when your body sleeps.
Everything you did
is sealed with sweet and sticky sap
to the marrow of my soul.
Everything you said
is caged in my mind
as I try to make the past real
when it isn't, try to make yesterday
alive, while it's dying with your flesh.

                    *

I think about what I'll give you -
the diamond necklace your father gave
me, crystal glasses in the china closet,
and my mother's silver star ring
that you took from my dresser
last year.   But I feel you over me,
laughing, and I know it's ridiculous
to think of these things
when you aren't really dying, just
changing spaces the way salmon
swim to the sea
before returning upstream
to start the cycle of life again.

                    *

My tears grow fierce like a desert storm
the second your spirit is free. I am weak
from the poisonous plague
that steals a slice of my soul

with creation's climax.

*

The way we were and the way it
was with you, my blue-eyed blond,
lives as a brief breath in eternity
now that you are gone.

*

Today I envy ten years ago,
when life hungered
for free space and future.
If I could only stand in the rain
and let it rinse away
this swollen Spring,
I would surrender to the miracles
of incarnated days
when there wasn't time.
I wouldn't think about tomorrow
or dust and dirty dishes.
I would choke life
with my love and learn each one
of those dumb blond jokes you told me
rather than be
seduced by poetry.

*

From your bedroom
I hear the eerie whine
under a full moon
and remember Midnight, your cat
disappeared so that
coyotes could celebrate lunch.
I see night decorated

with empty shadows that loom
over your marble Buddha
and Nirvana poster. I wonder
if your last words to me,
"I love you, too," will fade
with the dress I caress.   I feel
the hollow spot and close the door
to a living tomb that silently sears

---my heart forever.

W a k in g   U p

I wake up just in time to see
a dove sitting the wall, waiting

for fog to burn.   Still as the dead
breeze, it stares into space

that belongs to me before the sun
sprays the hill that watches

over shadows in the valley
and the old palm tree.

When the gray bird surrenders
to dying fog, I feel the great alone

while the shell of a snail on the rail
mocks holes in my green plant. Then,

sun exposes eucalyptus leaves
that shine in the light, and I wait

through the vacant day
soaked with sorrow

for mist to shroud the hills
again and swallow black birds

in the hollow dusk,
the way a girl wearing my love

glides around my memory world
and reveals the price
                    of golden dawns and stainless skies.

Thinking of Candice A. Lindsay 1980-1997

Counting The Shadows

My daughter is dead
And he's counting tree shadows,
The judge who's deciding
If justice is fed.

He's so fully bewitched
By a green pepper tree,
He can shut out sweet love,
That was stolen from me.

His circus performs
Each day as I sit,
And all I detect are
Remarks meant as wit.

But nothing is clever
When trees on a road
Deliver the death toll
To part of my soul.

And today's courtroom hearing
Can't hear me at all,
Because it's still wearing
A shapeless black shawl.

And no one around
The judicial arcade,
Can ever imagine

The pain of love severed

      When counting tree shadows
      Is worth a bench hour.

I Hear The Coyotes Cry Again

The savage, passing the house in the dark
knowing this is the night for garbage cans,
has no fear, but I shake from his stalking walk
and wonder if rabbits are awake. Candice
would probably lure him to her, the way
she could nurse and love frogs or kangaroo rats.
She didn't hate animals in the canyon
who devoured pets. She said, "We took away
their food. We stole their land. What would you do
without a grocery store?"

There was wisdom in her words and art.

She drew perfect pictures of birds
and wolves that hang silent on the wall.
She would draw this vagabond coyote,
but not before guarding the wild one
in search of prey. I watch the head bob,
thinking how worried I'd be
if Candice were here now.
I go inside and tears come for my girl
who left me
before my love for her was done.

Like the animal expelled from his home,
I'm hunting for life

        when I hear the coyotes cry again.

R o o t s

"What am I?" she asked
and I said, "A girl."
She didn't like my answer
and asked again,
"But what AM I?"
I looked at her way of seeing reality
and told her she was
Dutch, English,
Cherokee Indian,
Hungarian, and Irish,
which she let me know was not right
because she had to tell about her heritage
when diversity reigned in school.
After explaining that she wasn't her body,
that lineage held no weight with the spirit,
I wondered how my little girl would
define her birthright.   She told the teacher,
the truth, but the teacher ordered her
to pick just one branch from her roots,

so my blue-eyed blond

was a Cherokee Indian.

Part IV

From Life

Border Patrol

Sunglasses and a gun
decorate the special men
who stand in sizzling sun
wielding power with one hand
that dams the ocean freeway.

He feels the rays of Heaven
beat hard upon his head
so sleek green lawns
and the fortnight lily
can be nurtured
by those men
who smile for pay
that is given today;

       though the Border Patrol
       is appointed by law
       to take them away.

Slaughterhouse Ally

A woman
running with a child and a man,
(silhouettes
on the yellow freeway sign)
frames the ocean.
Cars and cars
full of people pass it,
but a mother died today
avoiding the checkpoint
and the border patrol
in a place we call
"Slaughterhouse Ally."
She'd made it before,
so she could have
the American dream
and I wondered why
she didn't walk
along the beach
instead of
Interstate Five.

Ritual

We sit in rows waiting,
Facing forward,
Silently ignoring
Polluted people,
While weekly cleansing
By merry Mexicans
Offers what saves us
From corrupted cars
At the carwash.

surplus

rows of pure cotton
wait in the sun
for the winter rains to come
when bales will go rotten
on the field
with migrant workers
summer yield

The Man Who Polishes the Golf Course

This morning,
a man sits on the steep, stony hill waiting.
His worn gray backpack is full
next to a water bottle that bakes in the sun.
A green Border Patrol van passes,
ignoring him and another brown man
on the barren bluff. They sleep in the canyon
while coyotes stalk cats from perfect neighborhoods
where flowers and bushes hem fences.
A truck stops and takes him to the place
where pros swing on velvet sod
he keeps alive as his skin turns darker.
He trims honeysuckle until noon,
when he sneaks across the valley
for lunch in the bushes.
A hard white ball bounces off his head,
but he has no complaint under the sun
that chases him to roads that carry a dream
day after day. His gaze turns reverent
when the sun is halved over the lagoon
where his shadow dances
near a truck of smiling Mexicans
with swollen pockets
who are divided at the corner

He has felt the land,
the man who wears a black baseball hat backwards,
and a smile when he crosses himself

and the border to Old Mexico.

Drain

Near Olde Ninety-Nine
Is a small town called Drain
Which some see as pleasant
And others say is plain,
But those who still live there
See mountains and trees,
Blackberries and fields,
And what's left of the air
That still breathes in clean.

In Fields Of Lavender

It's morning in the lavender fields
Inside the misty valley
Where a desert wind whispers
Between rows and rows of lavender
That Conquistadors once carried as scent
Against insects, and today baptizes life.

The oil from the bloom that anointed life
Inside sacred places asleep in pyramid fields,
Reaches a man who savors the scent
He planted between two mountains
To bestow flowers of white and purple
On a woman giving her child love whispers.

As the haze moves, the blossom whispers
Songs from Mediterranean life
When Julius Caesar carried the lavender
Far and away to the British fields
Where the candelabra spikes thrived in a valley
And filled the air with new perfume.

In the mist of war, the scent
Flew across a Flanders Field that whispers
Death in the shadows of a valley
Near the triumphant arch where people sprinkle life
With the perfume from green foliage in fields
Decorated with blooms of lavender.

The shades of lavender
Give medicine or tea a scent
That betrays the truth of the fields
And fills the air with swaying whispers
About creation that anoints life
And keeps the secret of the valley.

In the sunset, I walk through the valley
And see the rows of lavender
Sway in the wind and mist of life
Where air explodes with the sweet scent
Before the night moans with owl whispers
And coyotes whining in the fields.

The quiet of smoky fields carries tomorrow in the
                                             valley,
Whispers yesterday in the shadows of lavender,
And holds the scent today, a day that baptizes life.

Fat Harvey's Truck Stop

Fat Harvey's Truck Stop,
along a highway road,
where drivers find a special place,
to eat and rest and sing,
isn't fancy or expensive,
but it has a freedom ring,
for tired men who steal
free moments that are real.

Navy Pilot

His hair was dark as were his eyes,
A perfect form for women lies,
With unstained uniform of white,
And spit shined shoes reflecting light.

He clicked his heels and marched,
The stately ordained stomp,
And then stood square amid the pomp,
Saluting men with stars.

He stood thinking every day
Of ways to pull a teasing prank,
On commanders wearing medals,
And the symbols telling rank.

His thin lips held a hungry smile,
At the place where he made rate,
And stood at full attention,
Near the open gate.

He'd just finished flying school,
And held his Naval orders
To an aircraft warship
Full of shiny planes.

But just before he went to war,
To burst bombs from the air,
He stole one last embrace,
From a girl at her back door.

It worked the way the Captain planned,
Hour after hour, on Pacific seas,
Until one bullet hit the wing,
And forced his bomber to the sand.

There was no time to say a thing,
About the one he loved,
Whose fate was black of mourning
And not his wedding ring.

And at the grassy meadow,
Adorned with white, wood crosses,
He looked down and saw her,
Beside a weeping mother.

There was nothing left of him,
Except a flag and gun salute,
Presented with the rocket song,
That rang on far too long.

The bureaucratic agents then,
Preferred not to explain,
What happened to a Yankee plane,
Or one fearless flyer.

But I know where the pilot went,
After that short whining descent,
When I was born in forty-four,
A girl who vowed to never see war.

L o v e

Love is a walk in the bright sunlight
And talks very late on a stormy night.
It's fast food dinners and ice cream cones
That warm our hearts and chill our bones.
It's pecks on the cheek at the kitchen sink,
Or kisses with words and one little wink.
And love is a lady and man with a cane,
Who lived many days through sunshine and rain.
But love is also a man with his bride
Full of desire and hopeful pride.
And love is the innocent child's smile
Rewarding a mother and father awhile.
And love is a moment along the harbor
When a gray ship arrives with a sailor
Burning with yearning for his waiting girl
Who wears on her neck, a perfect pink pearl.
And love is full patience when squadrons pass by,
As Navy jets loudly descend from the sky
Before two lovers brimming with passion,
Connect and renew unbridled affection.
But most of all love is alive when we know
That every day is the day to sew
New strings of love where we freely give
A kind word and hug each day that we live.

The Crosses At Point Loma

Silence swallows sounds near the sea
where white monuments mock memorials
of wars that furnished freedom,
then raised exalted idols
along with empty soldier sleeves
and folded flags for those
who put flowers at the graves
where people on Point Loma pass,
but only see a pretty park
in dead designs of peace.

Iwo Jima

How soon people forget
The war
And that
If Marines had failed
To raise
The flag
On Mount Suribachi,
America
And Japan
Would have another
Story to Tell.

He Was A Marine

He wore full dress, with gloves and sword,
Looking like a royal lord,
This man who offered me his arm
And had a voice so full of charm.

I stood beside him feeling proud,
As people passed and slightly bowed
Near my Marine who walked so tall,
And took me with him to the ball.

And when the brass band played the song,
He stood attentive looking strong
Before he took me on his arm
To dance a waltz with noble charm.

And later in the celebration,
I sat teeming with elation,
At the birthday of the Corps,
Sure Marines saved me from war.

Stealth

The black, flat, delta wing,
a bomber with a freedom ring,
invented in strict secrecy
hid the truth the people could see
that shook not long ago,
the ground in San Diego.

The grand design of zealous men
comes from those who still don't tell,
if the number ten times ten
is the sum of silent jets made,
nor do they speak of where and when
the graves of many test pilots were laid
so we can honor those who paid
the price that surreptitiously saves.

The Sounds of War

The sounds of war
are in the sky
quaking earth beneath me
as A-6 jets
and Phantoms fly
all day and night above me
training for the deadline.

And at the harbor
gray ships float
away from land
and peaceful sand
with silver smart bombs
tucked inside,
while on the deck
boy soldiers stand,
as people on the shore
wave their flags and cheer
for dauntless warriors.

Yet those who take
the other side,
the ones who say
war's not okay,
celebrate with jeering
as they spew hate,
and burn a badge,
that symbolizes freedom.

After that it's very still
right here around the bay

and the moonlit city
where children sleep
in spite of bombs
secure upon the belly
of Navy fighter jets.

The First Gulf War begun by President GHW Bush

Coronado Bridge

The grand, noble arch
connects and severs people
from downtown.

La Jolla Cove

Low tide bares bald rocks
and pools of sea cucumber
are no longer free.

water

water flows
hunting for a place
to whirlpool

the drain is clogged

Part V

About Poetry and Other Things
A California Poet Thinks

I Saw The Poet

I saw the poet
summon artists to participate
in occasions of the state.
I was nervous for him
as he went out on a limb
that made "Stopping by Woods
On a Snowy Evening" seem warm.
It was so cold that January day
when I heard him say
things I learned in school
could one day rule
over the golden age of poetry.
Somebody, I don't know who,
helped him when they knew
wind could make his pages fly
away from his hand to the sky.
He finished what he started
for President Kennedy
and not too long after,
I remember the rites of life
were said for Robert Frost,
who was alive when I studied
his songs of life. Back then
I had no idea the phrases
he wrote would become praises
in the eyes of more people
than Miss Menninga.
Today, I marvel at creation
as I look at another creator
who will be worth remembering

                                    tomorrow.

a poet's poem

the genealogy of words
creeps over the hill with the sun,
until generation after generation
is born.   then
the belly begs for dinner
that is devoured
so i can sit at the screen
where it doesn't seem
that writing poetry
steals another day.

one poet's door

i knocked on the door
with perfect glass designs,
but no one answered
so i found another door,
rich with lines and colors
that some in the ivory tower
scorned,
and when the door opened,
a man with a smile,
showed me in.   we
talked about how words
can smell, taste, feel,
hear, see, and touch things,
and the way
the academic mafia
can shut the poet out

The Ones Who Rule The World

They talk and walk
hanging promises in a lofty place.
They refuse to stalk freedom
or loiter in the aisle of peace
as they walk and talk
about a plan
sure to seduce my grandchildren
to a line that will bend
in the fading light of the world.
I wish a whispering wind
could vaporize the masquerade
that created a generation
of politicians
who hawk falsehoods
for position and power,
and an existence showered
with golden calves
for the ones who rule the world

                                    with war.

The Dutch Speak of Dikes

I've known about dikes:
My father told us about one that is older
      than the royal blood in my veins.

My soul has grown high and strong like the dikes.

I washed in the water of life when the dawn was red.
I lived on the hill and fell asleep to sounds of Whidbey
                                    Island wind.
I viewed the mountains and the skies above them.
I heard the songs of immigrants at Ellis Island
      saw it from New York City, and I've seen
      the Statue of Liberty turn bright in the sunrise.

I've known about dikes:
New dikes holding in the North Sea.

My soul has grown high and strong like the dikes.

Influenced by Langston Hughes

My 15 Minutes

When I walked into the white room,
my foot hit the embroidered chair
catapulting me to the black chair
with wheels that broke my fall,
but cracked artwork
I had shaped once upon a time.
The pain is so deep
I wonder if
fractured bones will haunt me again.
I wonder if
this is a sign that the end is near.
I wonder if
I should hurry up
and finish the memoir,
the poems in progress,
and my youtube adventure
designed to wake up
the living dead in America
and conceived to bequeath me
15 minutes of glory before I die.

Poetry

The poetry inside of me
That begs with rhyme to be,
Looks for space
In this life-time
And not some place
Posthumously.

In this volume c. a. lindsay captures the spirit of San Diego County, which includes a military community and a broad geographic diversity. Her poetry also touches the human soul in poems that were inspired by life.

A poet with literary (*Old Hickory Review, The Kit-Cat Review, Mobius*) as well as commercial (*Leatherneck, Magazine of the Marines, USA Today*) credits, Lindsay has won numerous awards including: First Place in the Diablo-Alameda Poetry Contest, National League of American Pen Women, The Jeanette Gould Maino Writing Award, the Dr. Joseph Garbarini Honorary Award, NLAPW La Jolla Poetry Award, a Della Crowder Miller Award, various poetry awards from NLAPW, California South, the Helen Sutton Booth National Memorial Poetry Award, and Lucidity Poetry Journal Award. She was Poet of the Week for Poetry Express and The Poetry Super Highway. She won Editor's Choice Award and "Poet of the Quarter" from Dr. Charles Cravy, President of the Society of American Poets (Georgia).

Lindsay's poetry has been included in month-long juried art shows at the Poway Center for the Performing Arts, Poway, the East County Performing Arts Center Juried Art Show, El Cajon, and the Remington Club in San Diego, California. She was guest Author for *Lynx Eye* at the LA Times Festival of Books. One of her framed poems was hung in the Drawing Room of Todd Lincoln's former home in D.C. Lindsay has read her poetry at Pasadena Conservatory of Music, a sponsored event of Tebot Bach and Golden West College Long Beach. In San Diego, California, she has been a poetry guest at the Inner Change, Better World Galleria, La Jolla Library, Casa de las Compana, Java Joes, Rancho Bernardo Kiwanis Club, StoneRidge Country Club, and Borders Bookstore. A Lindsay poem was read by Melody Hall at New York's West End Theatre,

Lindsay is a member of NLAPW La Jolla, the COAL Gallery in Carlsbad, California, and she is a long-time member of the Academy of American Poets.

www.ingramcontent.com/pod-product-compliance
Lightning Source LLC
Chambersburg PA
CBHW020626250626
47154CB00004B/1686